Peter Noever

DIE GRUBE
THE PIT

Aedes

*Katalog zu der Ausstellung DIE GRUBE
Herausgegeben von Aedes, Galerie und
Architekturforum, Kristin Feireiss, Berlin*

*Catalogue of the Exhibition THE PIT
Published by Aedes, Galerie und Architekturforum,
Kristin Feireiss, Berlin*

*Mitarbeit an Ausstellung und Katalog /
Collaboration in Exhibition and Catalogue:
Herta Fail, Kristin Feireiss, Verena Formanek,
Marianne Friedl, Ingrid Gazzari, Matthias Mulitzer,
Andrea Nussbaum, Veit Pedit, Ulrich Senoner,
Friedrich Zaunrieth, Hagen Zurl*

*Fotos / Photos: Ixy Noever, Katarina Noever, Peter Noever,
Barbara Rhode, Brian Spence, Peter Strobl, Gerald Zugmann*

Transport: Panalpina, Wien

*Während der Ausstellung ist der Film von
Andrea Schurian DIE GRUBE, 1988, zu sehen*

*The Film DIE GRUBE, 1988 by Andrea Schurian
will be shown during the Exhibition*

© Peter Noever, Wien 1991

ISBN 3-901127-01-1

Printed in Austria

Peter Noever

DIE GRUBE
THE PIT

BREITENBRUNN / BURGENLAND

Ausstellung / Exhibition

Aedes
Galerie und Architekturforum Berlin
S-Bahnbogen 600, 1000 Berlin 12
Tel. (030) 312 25 98

12. Februar – 9. März 1991
12th February – 9th March, 1991

Printed by F. Seitenberg Ges. m. b. H., Vienna

*Besonderen Dank für ihre Unterstützung
zur Realisierung der Ausstellung
und des Ausstellungskataloges*

*Special Thanks for their Support
in the Realization of the Exhibition
and the Catalogue*

*Bundesministerium für Unterricht und Kunst, Wien
Alexander Maculan, Wien
Österreichische Länderbank AG, Wien/Berlin
Readymix Beton AG, Ratingen*

*Gegenüberliegende Seite / Facing page:
Steinbruch-Gang bei Nacht, ausgebaggert ohne Stützmauern, 1972 / Quarry Passageway at Night, excavated without Retaining Walls, 1972*

EINE KULTSTÄTTE OHNE KULT

Es liegt drei Jahre zurück, vielleicht auch länger, als mich Peter Noever mit zu seiner „Grube" nahm. Ein sonniger Herbsttag, mildes Licht, das Burgenland, das ich nicht kannte, Peter Noever, den ich kaum kannte . . . und dann ein Ort nirgendwo, der sich, so angestrengt man es auch versuchen mag, einer auch nur annähernd authentischen Beschreibung entzieht, dem Zugriff auch.

Damals beschloß ich doch wenigstens den Versuch zu unternehmen, die Eigenheit und Unverwechselbarkeit dieses Ortes einzufangen, in einer Ausstellung widerzuspiegeln. Schon die verbale Annäherung an die „Grube" kann nur Details wiedergeben, erfaßt nie das Ganze: ein Landschaftsarchitekturprojekt, ein Steinbruch mit gestalteten Elementen, eine Kultstätte ohne Kult, ein Kraftfeld.

Zeit, das war für mich eine intensive Erfahrung der „Grube", hat hier ein anderes Maß, einen verlangsamten Rhythmus. Es gibt sie hier in verschwenderischer Fülle und dies seltsamerweise auch für ihren Schöpfer oder sagen wir weniger pathetisch, ihren Gestalter: Peter Noever, dem Ur-Mannsbild einer hektischen Kulturszene, in der er sich wie kein zweiter bewegt, gern auch mal um sich schlägt und mit dem Kopf durch die Wand geht ohne erwähnenswerte Blessuren davonzutragen. Dort, in der Grube wird auch er still, verlangsamt sich sein Rhythmus, der Ort seiner jahrzehntelangen Auseinandersetzungen – und sie ist noch nicht abgeschlossen – hat von ihm Besitz ergriffen.

Die Frage an eine Architekturgaleristin, welcher Anteil an diesem Projekt nun Architektur sei, ist genauso müßig wie die Überlegung, daß doch nur vergleichsweise wenige Menschen diesen fast magischen Ort sehen und erleben werden. Aber allein die Tatsache, daß es diese Stätte gibt, macht uns bewußt, wie wichtig es ist, daß man irgendwo solche Orte findet, von denen Kraft ausgeht, geprägt von der Natur und dem menschlichen Eingriff, entstanden in Jahrzehnten und geschaffen vielleicht für Jahrhunderte.

Kristin Feireiss

A CULT SITE WITHOUT A CULT

It's been three years, maybe even longer, since Peter Noever took me along to his "Pit". A sunny fall day, mild light, Burgenland, which I didn't know at all, Peter Noever, whom I hardly knew . . . and then this place in the middle of nowhere. A place that evades even the most vague description, no matter how one might try.

Still, I decided to at least make the attempt to capture something of the uniqueness and unmistakability of it, and to mirror it in an exhibition. Even a mere verbal approach to the "Pit" is only capable of listing details. It could never convey the whole idea: a project in landscape architecture, a quarry with design elements, a cult site without a cult, an energy field.

Time – that was an intense experience for me at the Pit. It has another measure there, a slower pace. It's available in wasteful abundance, and, strangely enough, it seems to favor the creator (of the Pit) as well – or, to put it less pathetically – its designer: Peter Noever, a man among men in the hectic cultural scene. In it he moves like no other, from time to time bursting out with fists forward, or putting his head through the wall – and walking away without wounds worth mentioning. In the Pit he also becomes quiet, his rhythms slow. This place of personal struggle – still not quite complete – has taken possession of him.

The question of which part of this project might be called architecture is at least as tiresome for the director of an architectural gallery as the thought that actually comparatively few people will ever see and experience firsthand this somehow magical place. But the simple fact that there are such places makes us aware of how important it is that one can find them – radiating their energy, marked by both nature and the human hand, resulting over the course of decades and very possibly created for centuries.

Kristin Feireiss

Translation Michael Huey

Die Grube mit Steinbruch-Gang unmittelbar nach der Ausbaggerung (Luftaufnahme), 1972 / The Pit with Quarry Passageway just after excavation (Areal View), 1972

TERRA NOEVER

Es ist schon geraume Zeit her, seit die Skulptur, eingeengt von den begrenzten figuralen Darstellungsmöglichkeiten, der Aura einer Ergänzung zur Architektur und der Trübsinnigkeit des bloßen Ausgestelltseins, über ihre Grenzen – gleich den antiken Erdspuren und Hügelgebilden – hinausgegangen und in die Landschaft hereingebrochen ist. Aber die Skulptur, die sich bemüht, den Ort neu zu bestimmen und so einen erweiterten Raum zu schaffen, hat sich in eine Ironie von ausweglosen Proportionen begeben. Mit der Ambition, mehr zu erreichen, sind ihre Möglichkeiten geringer geworden. Die Prinzipien der minimalistischen Kunst, wie hoch auch immer der Energieaufwand für ihre Vollendung sein mag, werden bedrängt durch eine einzige Frage, die je öfter beantwortet um so uninteressanter geworden ist: Wie vage kann ein Konzept sein, um der Kunst zu entsprechen?
Peter Noevers einfühlsame, tektonische Grube riskiert die Anwendung von „earth art", um sie zugleich einer Überprüfung zu unterziehen, der sie niemals standhalten könnte, der Überprüfung der Nutzung. Elegant und einfach, die graziösen historischen Formen einer Geometrie umfassend, nimmt Noever die künstlerische Herausforderung über die Ethik hinaus an und stillt das Verlangen, das der Minimalismus erweckt. Mit seiner exzentrisch prächtigen burgenländischen „Datscha" hat Noever nicht nur ein Gelände und ein Monument für den Betrachter, sondern eine Lebensstätte geschaffen. Der Unterschied in Noevers Arbeit ist, daß sie nicht die Grenzen der Skulptur, sondern die Grenzen der Architektur hinterfragt. Das künstlerische Wohnkonzept wird nicht ausgeschlossen, jedoch nur abgeschwächt in Betracht gezogen, tanzt zum elektrisierenden Tango des Lebens, schwebt zum Ritual.
Es gibt eine Fotografie des alten Weinkellers, zu dem Noevers Projekt sowohl eine Erweiterung wie auch eine Ergänzung bildet. Unter dessen Gewölbe ist axial von Tür zu Tür – von der Straße zur Natur – ein langer, langer Tisch. Dieser Tisch setzt die einleitende Komponente zu dieser Arbeit und schafft eine Linie, die nach Weiterführung verlangt. Sie verläuft sowohl als Linie, als pure Energie, die hindurchgeht durch die wundervollen, mächtigen Stützwände und den angrenzenden Erdwall, sowie als ein Ereignis, das den Ort mit einer festlichen Stimmung belebt. Auf dem Tisch dieser Fotografie sind eine Reihe von Flaschen und Gläsern zu sehen, unzählige Liter Wein von den umliegenden Weingär-

ten, Anregungen für Genuß und Freude. Flackerndes Kerzenlicht für die Nachtschwärmer, die draußen vor der Tür auf ihre Einladung warten. Noevers Ort existiert in einer unentbehrlichen Konstellation zu den Aktivitäten, die er anregt und unterstützt: Die Ruine dieser Bauwerke wird daher nicht nur aus zerbröckeltem Beton bestehen, sondern auch aus den Überresten dieser Flaschen und Gläser und dem fortdauernden anregenden Geruch dessen, was dort getrunken wurde.

Die gesamte Landschaft wird zur Drehscheibe dieser Nutzung. Die Toilette in einem anderen Teil der Anlage ist wohl das eleganteste Klosett im Freien, das es je in der Geschichte gab. Aus einem wunderschönen Messinghahn fließt das Wasser in einen Waschtisch, der an die Anmut eines Taufbeckens erinnert. Gedacht für zwei Personen, lädt das Klosett gleich einer doppelhalsigen Weinflasche zu gemeinsamer Benützung ein. Zugleich ist diese Einrichtung auch anständig – nach all den Gläsern Sturm muß man nicht in den Wald pissen. Und in anderen sinnigen Momenten sitzt man in einem hinreißenden Raum und kann durch die Sehschlitze in die freie Landschaft spähen.

Ist diese Architektur nicht genial? Diese intime Verbindung einer alltäglichen aber doch absoluten Vision. Noever ist ein Meister der architektonischen Grundbegriffe, der Kunst des Grabens, Schneidens, Gießens und Stützens, der fundamentalen Rituale der Prozessionen über Auf- und Abgänge, dem Talent für Bindung und Erfassung der Situation, der offenen Ehrerbietung, die wir der Natur schulden; der transzendentalen Benutzung. Als vollendeter Architekt ermöglicht Noever es, den Körpern ein gelungenes Dasein in dieser Welt zu geben.

Den Formen der Zufriedenheit gewoben, erhebt er keine Einwendung gegen den Abbruch des Vorstellbaren. Unmißverständlich ist die Luftansicht der Grube der Spiegel der Venus. Aber damit sollte man sich nicht zu lange aufhalten, abgesehen von einer wesentlichen Tatsache: Noevers liebevolle Einschließung der beständigen Relevanz des Vertrauens.

Das ist Architektur. Innerhalb von ihrem Raum, ihrer Zeit und darüber hinaus, an wonnigen Nachmittagen und im Anblick der Mysterien der Kunst ist Peter Noevers Ort gesichert, unauslöschbar und von großer Schönheit.

Michael Sorkin

Michael Sorkin, geboren 1948, ist Architekt, Architekturprofessor und Architekturkritiker in New York

Übersetzung aus dem Englischen von Gabriele Kanner-Braunsberg

TERRA NOEVER

It's some time now since sculpture, hemmed by slackening figural possibilities, by the dimming aura of adjunction to architecture, and by boredom with just standing there, zipped out into the big open and – emulating ancient line carvers and mound builders – exceeded itself, bursting upon the landscape. But sculpture, remarking its sites to coopt an "expanded field" plunged itself into an irony of dead-end proportions. While it sought to do more, its means became less. The arts of minimalist punctuation, however mighty the energies necessary to achieve their monuments, were buggered by a single question that grew duller and duller as it was more and more answered: how small a concept will suffice to signify art.

Peter Noever's deft tectonic pit pulls earth art's singeing chestnuts out of the fire by confronting them with the test they could never abide, the test of use. Embracing the svelte historic forms of geometry elegant and simple, Noever assumes the art but spurns the ethic, slaking the thirst for more than Minimalism arouses. In his loopy magnificent Burgenland dacha, he has made not simply a site, an armature for spectatorship, but has crafted a place. Here's the difference: Noever's work tests not the edge of sculpture but the edge of architecture. The arts of habitation are not excluded but attenuated, made to dance to a langorous yet electric tango of life floated to ritual.

There's a photograph of the old wine cellar to which Noever's project forms both addition and completion. Under its vault, running axially from door to door – from street to nature – is a long, long table. This table is the initiating vector of the work, the line that begs extension. It continues both as line, pure energy, burrowing between gorgeous thick retaining walls through the hillock behind, and as event, suffusing the site with conviviality. On the table, in that photograph, lies a seriality of bottles and glasses, numberless litres of wine from the surrounding vineyards, injuctions to enjoyment. Candles flicker, revelers await invitation in, just outside the door. Noever's place exists in indispensable constellation with the activities it inspires and supports: the ruins of this place will properly entail not simply a crumbling of concrete but the shards of these bottles and glasses, and a pungent lingering aroma of all that was drunk there.

The pivot of use turns throughout. Elsewhere on the site is the toilet, easily history's most elegant outhouse. Wash water falls from a beautiful brass tap into a basin of baptismal grace. Nearby the toilet, a two holer. Like those serried plonk bottles, the two-ness of the thing invites a use that is, shall we say, collegial. And yet decorous: after all those glasses of sturm, one need not pee in the woods. And, at more contemplative moments, one sits in a ravishing space peering through its fissures to the landscape beyond, perfectly enframed.

Isn't this architecture's genius? This intimate union of the quotidian and the absolute vision. Noever's a master of the architectonic primary, of the arts of scooping, cutting, casting, retaining, of the fundamental rituals of procession, of ascent and descent, of the skills of attachment and situation, of the frank obeisances the natural is ever due, of transcendent use. Consummate architect, Noever invents happy ways for bodies to be in the world. And, friendly to the forms of contentment, he does not demur at the swift imprint of the imageable. Unmistakeably, the pit's airborne view's the mirror of Venus. No point in making too much of this save one thing: Noever's fond embrace of the abiding relevance of the familiar.

Here, then, is architecture. In and out of its place and time, about bee-buzzing afternoons as much as the conundrums of art, Peter Noever's place is assured, indelible, and very beautiful.

Michael Sorkin

Michael Sorkin, born 1948, is Architect, Professor of Architecture and Architecture Critic in New York

*Weinkeller, Grube, Steinbruch-Gang (Luftaufnahme), 1972 /
Wine Cellar, The Pit, Quarry Passageway (Areal View), 1972*

Weinkeller, Grube, Steinbruch-Gang, 1972 / Wine Cellar, The Pit, Quarry Passageway, 1972

SORTEN VON WAHRNEHMUNG

Konzepte mag Peter Noever nicht besonders. In Konzepten zu denken heißt für ihn, auf vergangene Erfahrungen angewiesen zu sein, Erklärungen liefern zu müssen. Noever stellt ihnen seine ,,Percepts" gegenüber, die ,,stark vom Spontanen, vom Sensorischen" getragen sind. Percepts schließen das Irrationale, den Zufall bewußt mit ein.
Der Inbegriff dieser Vorstellung scheint mir ,,Die Grube" zu sein, das Landschaftsarchitekturprojekt im burgenländischen Breitenbrunn, an dem Noever seit 1971 baut.
Ein altes Kellertor als Pforte der Wahrnehmung – dahinter, durch Jahrhunderte altes Gewölbe, durch die schützende Höhle aus der genetisch fixierten Erinnerung, tritt der Perzipient in das Kreisrund der Grube. Grobe Steinblöcke im Gras vor sich, die ansteigenden Kraterwände zu den Seiten, den zum Ausschnitt des Himmels reduzierten Rest der Welt über sich, packt ihn intuitive Erkenntnis: eine Kultstätte. Vielleicht wird hier gefeiert, was Architektur sonst nur noch selten vermittelt: Das Bauwerk als Produkt der Vereinigung von äußerer Umwelt und menschlichem Unbewußten. Erdwälle, Gänge und Mauern als äußere Markierungen eines magischen Orts.
Die Perzeption drängt sich einfach auf: ,,Stonehenge", jubelt der Betrachter beim Anblick des ,,Steinbruch-Ganges" der ,,Flügel-Treppen" und des ,,steinernen Klos", die den architektonischen Lehrpfad fortsetzen.
Doch Noever ist kein weltabgewandter Druide, den es ins östliche Österreich verschlagen hat. Als Designer und Museumsdirektor, als Querdenker in Zeiten, als dieses Etikett noch nicht erfunden war, schlägt er sich höchst diesseitig durch. Ob mit der schweren Machete im Dschungelkampf der österreichischen Bürokratie, ob mit der feinen Argumentationsklinge in den verbalen Duellen der Café-Society. Noever verläßt den Schauplatz solcher Gemetzel stets unverschwitzt. In seinen Augen läßt sich ein inneres Lachen perzipieren. Daß jene Baukünstler, die einst mit ihm gegen die Wiener Kommerzarchitektur auf die Barrikaden stiegen, inzwischen selbst kleine Tycoons geworden sind, amüsiert ihn nur. Zu Hans Hollein, nun Star der Szene, von dem die Äußerung kolportiert wurde, in Wien könne nichts gebaut werden, was er nicht dulde, formulierte Noever sarkastisch: ,,Weilt Hollein noch unter uns?"
Anlaß für größere Reibereien war Noevers Entwurf einer Betonplattform, der Extension des Gartens im Wiener Museum für angewandte Kunst, hineinragend ins Bett des Wien-

Flusses. Architekten, die den Museumsgarten gern mit Bauvolumen gefüllt hätten, machten einen Teil der Öffentlichkeit gegen das „Noever-Plateau" mobil. Der Gestalter, der zugibt, von der Suche nach Grenzbereichen fasziniert zu sein, deutet seine geschmähte Rampe in ähnlich ursprünglichen Kategorien wie seine Grube im Burgenland: Die Terrasse sei „eine Geste der Einladung", wie eine offene Hand; ein Zeichen, „in das man viele rationale Argumente einpacken kann". Als Gestalter ist der mit der Absurdität des Lebens Vertraute von tiefem Ernst.

Kritikern erschien der Plan dennoch als Gag, der aber nicht zum Lachen reizt, sondern würgend im Halse steckt: Der Direktor setze sich im Museumsgarten sein eigenes Denkmal.

Er gebe allen Kritikern Recht, umflutete Peter Noever seine Gegner mit milder Ironie. Denn „jede Arbeit wird aus Notdurft verrichtet", sagte er kürzlich in einem Interview. „Auch meine", fügte er mit Wiener Konzilianz, die er – zumindest im Gespräch – auch hat, hinzu.

Erhard Stackl

Erhard Stackl, geboren 1948 in Wien, ist Stellvertretender Chefredakteur des österreichischen Nachrichtenmagazins „profil"

TYPES OF PERCEPTION

Peter Noever doesn't especially like concepts. In his view, conceptual thinking means reliance on past experience . . . and having to make explanations. "Percepts" are Noever's answer to concepts. Theirs is the realm of "spontaneity and sensation".
The ultimate expression of this way of thinking seems to me to be "The Pit" – a landscape architecture project in Breitenbrunn/Burgenland that Noever has been working on since 1971.
An old wine cellar entrance is the gateway to wisdom: past which, as we wander through a centuries old vaulted chamber, through the proverbial protective cavern of our genetically coded memory, we enter the circular space of the quarry. Rough blocks of stone in the grass ahead, the steeply-climbing crater walls on all sides, the rest of the world above, reduced to the slice of visible sky – all this culminates in an innate awareness: this is a place of workship. And it still celebrates, perhaps, what contemporary architecture is seldom able to convey: the feeling that the construction is the product of a union between outward environment and human unconsciousness. Dirt embankments, passageways, and walls are the outward indications that this is a magical site.
The impression is unavoidable: "Stonehenge" comes to the viewer's mind as he examines the "Quarry Passageway", the "Wing-Stairs", and the stone outhouse – all of which are extensions along this architectural path of knowledge.
And yet Noever is no druid who has turned his back on the world-nor has he hidden himself away in easternmost Austria. As a designer and museum director, as a nonconformist in an age when this label hadn't yet been thought up, he's been highly effective in fighting his way over here. Whether it's with a huge machete in jungle warfare with the Austrian bureaucracy, or with subtly barbed arguments in the verbal duels of the cafe society. Noever never breaks a sweat on these battlefields. In his eyes you see inner laughter.
It only serves to amuse him that the architects who once climbed the ramparts with him against commercial architecture have in the meantime become small tycoons themselves. Of Hans Hollein, who is currently the star of the show – and whose statement made the rounds that nothing he disapproved of could be built in Vienna – Noever has sarcastically posed the question: "Is Hollein still with us?"

Cause for even greater tension was Noever's design for a concrete platform, the extension of the courtyard of Vienna's Museum for Applied Arts out over the bed of the Vienna River. Architects who would have preferred to fill up the museum courtyard with structures mobilized a group from the public against the "Noever Plateau". The designer, who admits his fascination for testing boundaries, places his infamous ramp in an original category similar to that of his pit in Burgenland: the terrace is "an inviting gesture", like an open hand; a symbol "into which one could interpret a variety of rational arguments". As designer, he is extremely serious – despite his familiarity with the absurdity of life.

Nonetheless, critics believed the plan to be a gag that they didn't find very funny – one that stuck in their throats, in fact: the director was erecting his own memorial in the museum courtyard.

Peter Noever disarmed his opponents with mild irony: he agreed with the critics. For, "every project is done to satisfy one's own needs", he said recently in an interview. "Mine is no exception", he added with Viennese amiability, which – at least in discussion – he also possesses.

Erhard Stackl

Erhard Stackl, born in 1948 in Vienna, is the deputy editor in chief of the Austrian news magazine "profil"
Translation Michael Huey

Die Grube, 1973 / The Pit, 1973

Lageplan / Site Plan

Der Turm / The Tower   Beton-Steine /
Concrete Rocks

Steinbruch-Stiegenanlage /
Quarry-Stair Construction

Flügeltreppen /   Klosett mit Beton-Plateau /
Wing-Stairs   Toilet with Concrete Plateau

Steinbruch-Gang /
Quarry Passageway

Holz-Plateau /   Die Grube /
Wood-Plateau   The Pit

Weinkeller / Wine Cellar

Der Turm / The Tower

Beton-Steine /
Concrete Rocks

Steinbruch-Stiegenanlage /
Quarry-Stair Construction

Klosett mit Beton-Plateau /
Toilet with Concrete Plateau

Flügeltreppen /
Wing-Stairs

Steinbruch-Gang /
Quarry Passageway

Holz-Plateau /
Wood-Plateau

Die Grube /
The Pit

Weinkeller / Wine Cellar

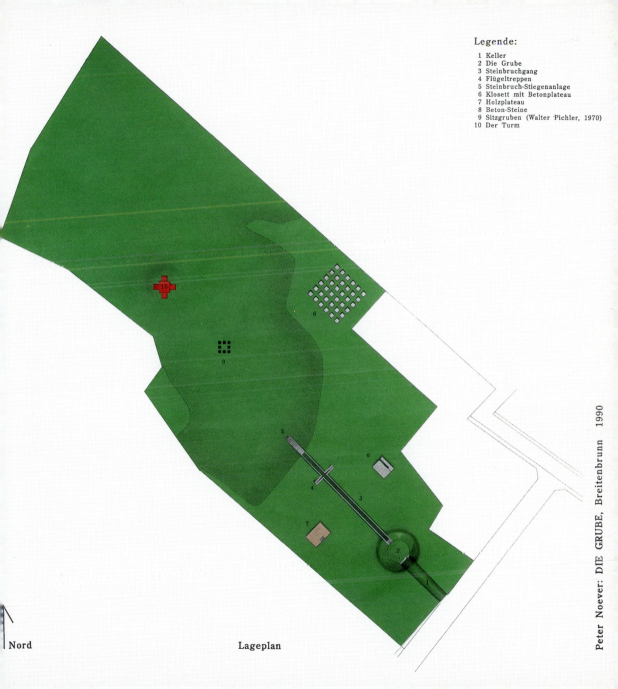

*Die Ortschaft Breitenbrunn vor 1945 /
The Village of Breitenbrunn before 1945*

DIE GRUBE – CHRONOLOGIE EINES PROJEKTES

1971	*Adaptierung des bestehenden 200 Jahre alten, burgenländischen Weinkellers*
Bauphase I 1972/73	*Bau der Grube (in Zusammenarbeit mit Werner Schalk) und Ausbaggerung des über 65 m langen und 3,5 m hohen unterirdischen ,,Steinbruch-Ganges"*
Bauphase II 1977	*Errichtung einer 15 m langen und 3,5 m hohen Beton-Stützmauer (im Anschluß an die Grube), beidseitig, zur Einfassung des vorhandenen ,,Steinbruch-Ganges"*
Bauphase III 1980/81	*Errichtung der Anschluß-Stützmauern (50 m Länge) und Fertigstellung des ,,Steinbruch-Ganges" mit weißgekalkten Beton-Wänden. Bau von 2 ,,Flügel-Treppen" und der ,,Steinbruch-Stiegenanlage"*
Bauphase IV 1982/83	*Bau des ,,Klosetts mit Beton-Plateau" (Entwurf 1980), in den Hang gebaut, parallel zur Grubenanlage. Trocken-Klosett in schalreiner Betonausführung mit ,,Estraden-Sitz" für 2 Personen und Waschnische mit Fließwasser (Gesamtfläche 70 m²)*
1985	*Entwurf des Projektes ,,Haus-Fragment" (nicht realisiert – anstelle dessen 1990 36 ,,Beton-Steine" errichtet)*
1986	*Errichtung des ,,Holz-Plateaus" (70 m²) parallel zur Gruben-Anlage*
1990	*Ausbaggerung und Herstellung des Platzes für die 36 ,,Beton-Steine" (220×220×120 cm, je 3,5 Tonnen), Errichtung der Fundamente und Aufstellung*
1990/91	*Entwurf und Planung ,,Der Turm" (6×6 m Grundfläche, Höhe 25 m). Herstellung verschiedener Arbeitsmodelle (Karton, Holz, Eisen)*

1972 erfolgte die Freilegung der Rückseite des 200 Jahre alten burgenländischen Weinkellers in Verbindung mit dem Bau der trichterförmigen Grube (Durchmesser 8 m, Trichteröffnung 20 m, Höhe 8 m, Neigungswinkel etwa 53°).
Bereits ein Jahr vorher wurde der aus Sandstein (des angrenzenden Steinbruchs)

bestehende und mit einem bewachsenen Dach ausgebildete Weinkeller (30 m Länge, 5 m Breite) renoviert.

Durch das Einziehen einer Trennungsmauer im Keller entstand zusätzlich ein zur Grube geöffneter und mit dem ursprünglichen Kellergewölbe gedeckter Raum: Schutz vor extremer Hitze; Schutz bei Regenwetter. Die Bänke und Tische, ebenfalls aus Sandstein, welche mit dem Boden bzw. dem Kellergewölbe verbunden sind, wurden dazu gebaut. Die Tischsockel und Steinbänke sind wie sämtliche andere Steinteile des Weinkellers weiß gekalkt. Die gesamte Fläche des Kellerbodens wurde mit alten Bauziegeln ausgelegt. Die nun vorhandene Eingangstür in massivem Kirschholz wurde 1982 eingebaut.

Abgesehen von allen anderen Aspekten und Anliegen wurde, um von der Grube einen Zugang (und Ausblick) auf den zum Weinkeller gehörenden Steinbruch zu haben, ein 65 m langer, 3,5 m hoher ,,Steinbruch-Gang" (eingefaßt mit einer 40 cm starken, weiß gekalkten Beton-Stützmauer) errichtet. Der ,,Steinbruch-Gang" mündet in die ,,Steinbruch-Stiegenanlage", welche in das ca. 15 m tiefer liegende Steinbruch-Gelände führt. Sowohl die ,,Steinbruch-Stiegenanlage" als auch der ,,Steinbruch-Gang" liegen exakt auf der Kellerachse.

Die zwei weithin sichtbaren ,,Flügel-Treppen"-Elemente sind etwa 15 m vor Beginn der ,,Steinbruch-Stiegenanlage" situiert und ermöglichen nach beiden Seiten den Zugang zur freien Landschaft sowie zum ,,Klosett mit Beton-Plateau", dem ,,Holz-Plateau" und zu den 36 ,,Beton-Steinen".

Von der Seite betrachtet sind die Grube und der ,,Steinbruch-Gang" (bewachsene Böschung) eine kontinuierliche Weiterführung des Kellerdaches (bewachsene Erde und gleiche Höhe). Damit, und durch die anderen, sorgfältig bedachten Maßnahmen wurde die Gruben-Anlage organisch in die Landschaft eingebunden und setzt dennoch der Natur einen gebauten Akzent gegenüber.

Das ,,Klosett mit Beton-Plateau" ist ein unabhängiger Baukörper, der erste von einer Reihe geplanter Baukörper und ähnlicher Maßnahmen, und ist von der Grube über den ,,Steinbruch-Gang" und eines der ,,Flügel-Treppen"-Elemente erreichbar. Die Klosett-Anlage ist in den Hang gebaut und weist im weitesten Sinn Analogien zur Gruben-Anlage auf (Gangsituation, Treppenelemente, die zum Klosett-Sitz führen . . .). Die Anordnung dieses Beton-Baukörpers (nicht gekalkt, schalreine Betonausführung) erfolgt parallel zur Gruben-Anlage.

Das ,,Haus-Fragment", geplant 1985, bestehend aus drei parallel angeordneten ca. 25 m langen und etwa 7 m hohen Ziegel-Mauern und -Säulen (verputzt und weiß gekalkt) und den mittleren Elementen mit einer Höhe von ca. 12 m, wurde nicht realisiert. Anstelle

dessen entstand an dem dafür vorgesehenen Ort die Anlage mit den 36 ,,Beton-Steinen". Das ,,Holz-Plateau", 1986 errichtet, ist eine massive, stegartige Holzkonstruktion, ca. ½ m über dem Bodenniveau liegend, und über eine Holzstiege zugänglich. Das ,,Holz-Plateau" liegt exakt gegenüber dem ,,Klosett mit Beton-Plateau". Durch diese Situierung ergibt sich ein bestimmter Blickwinkel sowohl seitlich auf die Klosett-Anlage als auch auf die Anlage mit den 36 ,,Beton-Steinen".
Das nächste zur Realisierung vorgesehene Projekt ist ,,Der Turm". Der Standort dafür befindet sich auf einem Hügel im Inneren des Steinbruch-Geländes. Die Position des Turmes bricht die Symmetrie der gesamten Anlage und ist exakt nach den vier Himmelsrichtungen ausgerichtet. Der Bauplatz für den Turm erinnert gleichzeitig an die erste ,,Besitzergreifung" des Geländes 1970 (durch Errichtung eines Tisches und einer Bank aus Holz an dieser Stelle).

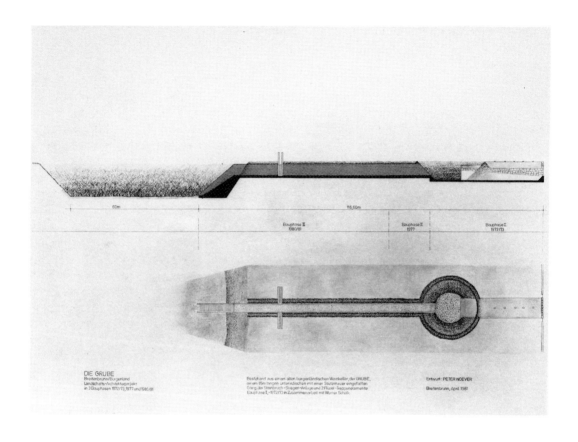

Die Grube, 1981 / The Pit, 1981

THE PIT – CHRONOLOGIE OF A PROJECT

1971	Adaptation of the existing 200 years old traditional wine cellar
Stage I 1972/73	Construction of "The Pit" (in cooperation with Werner Schalk) and excavation of an Underground "Steinbruch-Gang" ("Quarry Passageway") – more than 65 m long and 3.5 m high
Stage II 1977	Erection of a Concrete Retaining Wall, almost 15 m long and 3.5 m high (connecting with the Pit) to enclose both sides of the existing "Steinbruch-Gang" ("Quarry Passageway")
Stage III 1980/81	Construction of the Connecting Retaining Walls (50 m long) and completion of the "Steinbruch-Gang" ("Quarry Passageway") with white-washed concrete walls. The two "Flügel-Treppen" ("Wing-Stairs") and the "Steinbruch-Stiegenanlage" ("Quarry-Stair Construction") under construction
Stage IV 1982/83	The "Klosett mit Beton-Plateau" ("Toilet with Concrete Plateau") being built (designed in 1980) into the slope parallel to the Pit Construction. A toilet-without-flush in concrete including a washing-niche with running water (total area 70 sq m)
1985	Project "Haus-Fragment" ("House-Fragment") – not realized – instead of this 1990, 36 "Beton-Steine" ("Concrete Rocks") erected
1986	Erection of the "Holz-Plateau" ("Wood-Plateau" – 70 sq m) parallel to the Pit construction
1990	Excavation and construction of the site for the 36 "Beton-Steine" ("Concrete Rocks" – 220×220×120 cm, each one 3.5 tons). Construction of the foundations and setting up
1990/91	Design and planning of "Der Turm" ("The Tower" – base 6×6 m, height 25 m). Making of various work-models (Cardboard, Wood, Steel)

In 1972 work began on the funnel-shaped Pit (diameter 8 m, funnel opening 20 m, height 8 m, slope about 53°) by exposing the rear of the more than 200 years old traditional wine cellar.

One year prior to this, in 1971, the wine cellar (30 m long, 5 m wide) had been renovated and adapted to the new demands. The wine cellar is of sandstone (from the bordering Quarry) and is covered with a grass roof.

Through the construction of a dividing wall in the cellar an additional room facing the Pit and covered by the original vaulted ceiling was gained, thus offering protection from extreme heat and rain. The benches and tables consisting of sandstone were built and integrated into the existing substance of floor and vaulted ceiling. The table base and stone benches are white-washed as are all other stone elements of the wine cellar. The entire cellar floor is tiled with old bricks. The now existing entrace-door made of solid cherry-wood, was built-in, in 1982.

Apart from all other aspects a 65 m long and 3.5 m high "Steinbruch-Gang" ("Quarry Passageway" – enclosed by a 40 m thick, white-washed Concrete Retaining Wall) was built to enable access from the Pit (as well as a view) to the Quarry. This passing axis (the wine cellar being part of it) is determined by the continuation of the "Steinbruch-Stiegenanlage" ("Quarry-Stair Construction") leading into the open quarry grounds – approx. 15 m lower to the "Steinbruch-Gang" ("Quarry Passageway"). The "Steinbruch-Stiegenanlage" ("Quarry-Stair Construction") as well as the "Steinbruch-Gang" ("Quarry Passageway") are located on the axis of the cellar plane.

The "Flügel-Treppen-Elemente" ("Wing-Stair Elements") are situated approximately 15 m in front of the beginning of the "Steinbruch-Stiegenanlage" ("Quarry Stair Construction") providing access from both sides to the open, as well as to the "Klosett mit Beton-Plateau" ("Toilet with Concrete Plateau"), the "Holz-Plateau" ("Wood-Plateau") and the 36 "Beton-Steine" ("Concrete Rocks").

Seen from the side the Pit and the "Steinbruch-Gang" ("Quarry Passageway" – overgrown embankment) continue the line of the cellar roof (overgrown ground at the same height). Through these carefully considered measures, the Pit Construction was fitted into the landscape while at the same time still representing a contrast to it.

The "Klosett mit Beton-Plateau" ("Toilet with a Concrete Plateau") is an independent construction, the first realized out of a series of planned constructions. It can only be reached from the Pit by descending the "Steinbruch-Gang" ("Quarry Passageway") and climbing up one side of the "Flügel-Treppen-Elemente" ("Wing-Stair Elements"). The toilet site is built into the slope and in a sense consists of similar features as the Pit Construction (the arrangement of the Passageway, Staircase Elements that lead to the toilet seat . . .); the positioning of this concrete module (not white-washed, original concrete) is parallel to the Pit-Site.

Not implemented, was the, in 1985 originally planned "Haus-Fragment" ("House-Fragment"), which would have consisted of three parallel brick walls of some 25 m length and 7 m height, as well as brick columns (plastered and white-washed) and also the central elements with a projected height of some 12 m. In its place, and in the location, the site with the 36 "Beton-Steine" ("Concrete Rocks") was built.

The "Holz-Plateau" (Wood-Plateau") built in 1986, is a massive footbridge-like timber construction which lies approximately 0.5 m above ground-level, accessible through wooden steps. The location offers a given angle of view, both towards the side of the toilet site and the site with the 36 "Beton-Steine" ("Concrete Rocks").

The next project to be realized is "Der Turm" ("The Tower"). Its location will be on a hill on the side of the quarry. The positioning of "Der Turm" ("The Tower") will break the symmetry of the site and points exactly in the four geographic directions. The building-site, for "Der Turm" ("The Tower") reminds one at the same of the first taking-into-possession of the site in 1970 (by setting up, there, a table and a bench made of wood).

Translation Simon Quijano-Evans

Weinkeller, Grube, Steinbruch-Gang, Flügel-Treppen-Elemente, Steinbruch-Stiegenanlage, 1981, Klosett mit Beton-Plateau, 1983 (Luftaufnahme) / Wine Cellar, The Pit, Quarry Passageway, Wing-Stair Elements, Quarry-Stair Construction, 1981, Toilet with Concrete Plateau, 1983 (Areal View)

Die Grube (Luftaufnahme). Im Vordergrund Steinbruch-Stiegenanlage / The Pit (Areal View). In the foreground, Quarry-Stair Construction

Vorderansicht des alten burgenländischen Weinkellers / Front View of the old Wine Cellar

Blick vom Weinkellerdach in das Steinbruch-Gelände, 1981 / View from the Roof of the Wine Cellar in the Quarry Area, 1981

Weinkeller, Innenansicht / Wine Cellar, Interior View

Blick vom Weinkeller in die Grube / View from the Wine Cellar into the Pit

Blick in das Kellergewölbe mit gemauerten Tischen und Bänken; Tischplatten aus Sandstein / View into the Cellar with walled-in Tables and Benches; The Table-Tops are made of Sandstone

Kellertür zur Grube aus Kirschholz, 1975 / The Door of the Cellar made of Cherry-Wood, 1975

Die Grube mit Sandstein-Blöcken und Sandstein-Stiege / The Pit with Blocks of Sandstone and Sandstone Stairs

Steinbruch-Gang mit Flügel-Treppen-Elemente / Quarry Passageway with Wing-Stair Elements

Kreuzungspunkt—Ausstieg aus dem Steinbruch-Gang / Cross Point—Exit from the Quarry Passageway

1. November 1981: Einsturz einer über 30 m langen Stützmauer im Steinbruch-Gang während der Bauarbeiten
Kurz vorher: Photoaufnahmen für das Jahresplakat „Verschüttet . . .", bereits damals prophezeite der burgenländische Arbeiter, der Erde auf den Kopf von P. N. zu schütten hatte, Unglück.

November 1st, 1981: Collapse of a more than 30 m long Retaining Wall in the Quarry Passageway during the Construction Work
Just before: Shooting the Photo for the New Year Poster "Buried Visions . . ." previously the worker, who had to pile earth on the head of P. N., prophesied misfortune.

*Innenansicht der zwei Flügel-Treppen /
Interior View of the two Wing-Stairs*

Flügel-Treppen / Wing-Stairs

Flügel-Treppen / Wing-Stairs

Flügel-Treppen. Im Hintergrund Klosett mit Beton-Plateau / Wing-Stairs. In the background, Toilet with Concrete Plateau

Steinbruch-Stiegenanlage. Im Hintergrund die Ortschaft Breitenbrunn und der Neusiedlersee / Quarry-Stair Construction. In the background, the Village of Breitenbrunn and the Neusiedlersee

Detail der Steinbruch-Stiegenanlage / Detail of the Quarry-Stair Construction

Steinbruch-Stiegenanlage – Abgang in den Steinbruch / Quarry-Stair Construction – Exit to the Quarry

Blick vom Bauplatz des Turmes auf Breitenbrunn / View from the Site of the Tower over Breitenbrunn

„... eine Auseinandersetzung mit einem faszinierenden Ort, ein schrittweise vollzogener Denk- und Arbeitsprozeß, dessen Logik nur vor Ort verstanden werden kann. Das Landschafts-Architektur-Projekt ‚Die Grube' versammelt ein beachtliches Potential von Verliebtheit in einen Ort und von Aggression zur Selbstbehauptung."

" ... a dialogue with a fascinating place, an intellectual and building process developed gradually step by step, whose logic can only be comprehended through an understanding of the place. The land-art-project 'The Pit' contains a considerable potential of amorousness in a place as well as enough aggressiveness to be culminating in sheer self-determination."

Friedrich Achleitner, 1983

„Hier in Breitenbrunn ist nicht nur ‚Land-Art' entstanden, hier sind bauliche Sehnsüchte verwirklicht, die wir uns nicht eingestehen dürfen ..."
„... Keller, Grube und Pfad: ein kultischer Ablauf, ein neues, gläubiges Heidentum, sakrale Würde (die uns die aufgeklärten Religionen heute verweigern) bis an die Grenze des Pathos: trotzdem, nein, eben deswegen so wunderbar zum Feiern und zur Sentimentalität: Feuer, Wein, Brot (mit allerhand drauf), Freunde, Gespräche, Snobismus, Banalität, Austausch, Traurigkeit, Berauschtheit."

"Not only 'land-art' but rather building dreams that we are not used to confessing have been realized here in Breitenbrunn ..."
" ... Cave, pit and path: a ritual course, a new, devout paganism. Sacral dignity (denied us by enlightened religion as of today) nearly bordering on pathos: nevertheless, not just because it is ideal for celebrations and sentimentality: fire, bread (with lots of things on top) and wine, friends, conversations, snobism, banality, exchange, sadness, intoxication."

Günther Feuerstein, 1986

Begegnung in der Grube / Encounters in the Pit
Carlo Scarpa, 1973, und/and Bernard Rudofsky, 1977

„Ein österreichisches Lusthaus, ein offenes Labyrinth, von einem Meister des Understatements mit Wiener Eleganz inmitten von Weinbergen gebaut."

"An Austrian Folly, an open labyrinth, set with Viennese elegance into a vinous landscape by a master of understatement."

Bernard Rudofsky, 1988

«... una semplice arguta immagine offerta all'amicizia – stonehenge ritrovata – pronto a raccogliere nell'arco del cielo nouve forme per voi per noi ...»

„... eine schlichte, geistvolle Darstellung, der Freundschaft gewidmet – neuentdecktes Stonehenge –, bereit, neue Formen vom Himmelsbogen zu holen für Euch, für uns ..."

"... a simple, witty and ingenious figuration, rendered for friendship – Stonehenge regained – ready to take in the vault of heaven, new forms for you and for us ..."

Carlo Scarpa, 1973

Birnbaum mit Tisch und Bank aus Eichenholz und Nußholz / Pear-Tree with Table and Bench made of Oak- and Walnut-Wood

Detail des Tisches und der Bank / Detail of Table and Bench

Holz-Plateau 70 m², 1986 / Wood-Plateau 70 sq m, 1986

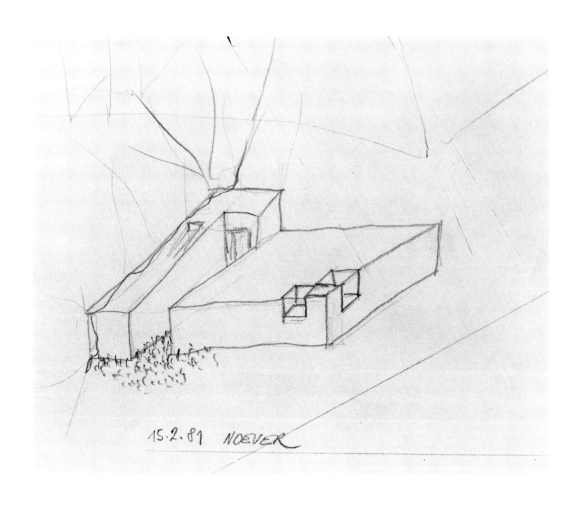

Klosett mit Beton-Plateau, Entwurf 1981 / Toilet with Concrete Plateau, Project 1981

Klosett mit Beton-Plateau, Realisierung 1983 / Toilet with Concrete Plateau, Realization 1983

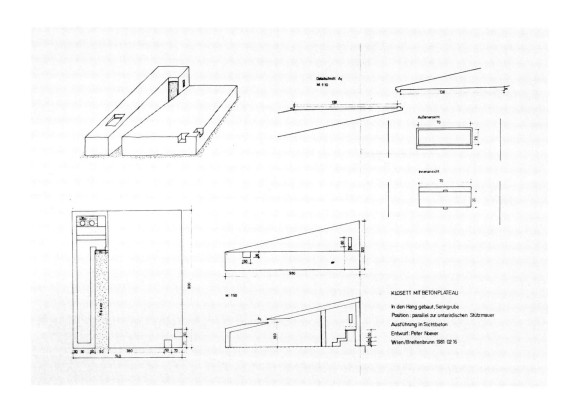

Klosett mit Beton-Plateau, Konstruktionszeichnung mit Details, 1981 / Toilet with Concrete Plateau, Drawing with Details, 1981

Wasserhahn aus Messing / Brass Tap

Waschbecken aus Beton mit integrierter Seifenablage / Wash-Basin, with integrated Soap Holder, made of Concrete

Klosett mit Beton-Plateau / Toilet with Concrete Plateau

Zwei Sitze für die Wartenden im Beton-Plateau / Two Waiting-Seats in the Concrete Plateau

Innenansicht des Klosetts mit Beton-Plateau. Sehschlitz mit Blick auf den Steinbruch / Interior View of the Toilet with Concrete Plateau. Observation Slit with View over the Quarry

Trockenklosett mit ,,Estraden-Sitz" für zwei Personen / Toilet without Flush in Concrete boarding with a Seat (of Estrade) for two Persons

Klosett mit Beton-Plateau, Schalungs- und Betonierarbeiten, 1982

Toilet with Concrete-Plateau, Form- and Concrete Work, 1982

Fest in der Grube, 1973 / links oben 1989

Gathering in the Pit, 1973 / page 62 in the upper left: 1989

Erd- und Bauarbeiten des 65 m langen unterirdischen Steinbruch-Ganges und Errichtung der Anschlußstützmauern, 1980

Excavation and Construction of the 65 m long Underground Quarry Passageway and the Connecting Retaining Walls, 1980

Fertigstellung der Steinbruch-Stiegenanlage und des Steinbruch-Ganges, 1981 / Completion of the Quarry-Stair Construction and the Quarry Passageway, 1981

Aufstellung der 36 Beton-Steine (220×220×120 cm, je 3,5 Tonnen) im Winter 1989/90

Setting up of the 36 Concrete Rocks (220×220×120 cm, each one 3.5 tons), Winter 1989/90

36 Beton-Steine für die von Peter Noever gestaltete Ausstellung „Land in Sicht" in Mücsarnok, Budapest, April/Mai 1989
„... Das Betonobjekt nimmt Bezug auf sechs Säulen der Museumsfassade und überträgt deren Rhythmus in eine räumliche Struktur, das so abgesteckte Terrain bildet für die Dauer der Ausstellung einen neuen Schwerpunkt, eine Irritation des Platzgefüges. Ein unbestimmtes Ereignis signalisierend erfährt das Objekt nachts die eigentliche Funktion: Aus 36 in die einzelnen Quader integrierten Lautsprechern wird der Ton zur Außenprojektion zugespielt..."
Herbst 1989, Ankauf der Beton-Steine durch Peter Noever, um sie auf dem für das „Haus-Fragment" vorgesehenen Bauplatz aufzustellen

36 Concrete Rocks for the Exhibition, "Land in Sicht" designed by Peter Noever in Mücsarnok, Budapest, April/May 1989
"... The Concrete Object relates itself to six columns of the Museum's front, and translates their rhythm into a spatial structure; the thus marked out terrain forms a new centre of gravity for the duration of the exhibition, an irritation of the site-structure. Heralding an uncertain event, the Object comes to realize its real function, at night: Sound comming out of 36 loudspeakers built into the individual stones..."
Autumn 1989, purchase by Peter Noever of the Concrete Rocks, for setting up on the building site foreseen for the "House-Fragment"

36 Beton-Steine im Steinbruch-Gelände, 1990 / 36 Concrete Rocks in the Quarry Area, 1990

Műcsarnok, Budapest,
Ausstellung ,,Land in Sicht"
Im Vordergrund das Betonobjekt (Fotomontage) /
Műcsarnok, Budapest
Exhibition "Land in Sicht"
In the foreground, the Concrete Object (montage)

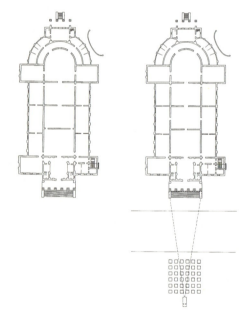

Die Ausstellungsräume des Műcsarnok und
Adaptation für die Ausstellung ,,Land in Sicht" /
The Exhibition rooms of the Műcsarnok and
Adaptation for the Exhibition "Land in Sicht"

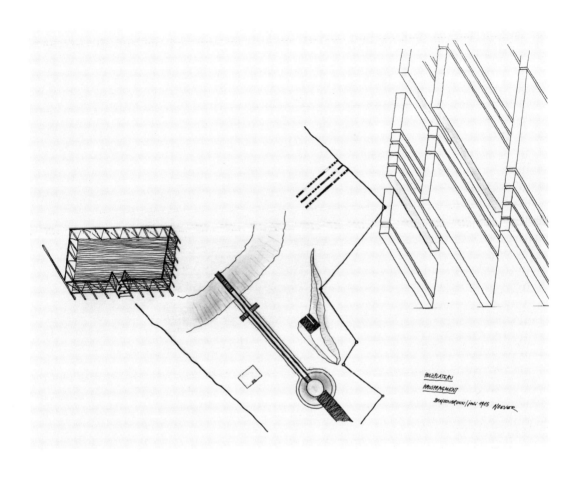

Zwei Projekte: Holz-Plateau und Haus-Fragment, 1985 / Two Projects: Wood-Plateau and House Fragment, 1985

Der Turm, Nordansicht, Projekt 1990, Grundfläche 6×6 m, Grundfläche mit Flügelkörper 12×12 m, Höhe 25 m (Modell aus massivem Eisen, Maßstab 1:33, Höhe 76 cm) / The Tower, form North Side View, Project 1990, base 6×6 m, base with Wing-bodies 12×12 m, height 25 m (model of solid steel, scale 1:33, height 76 cm)

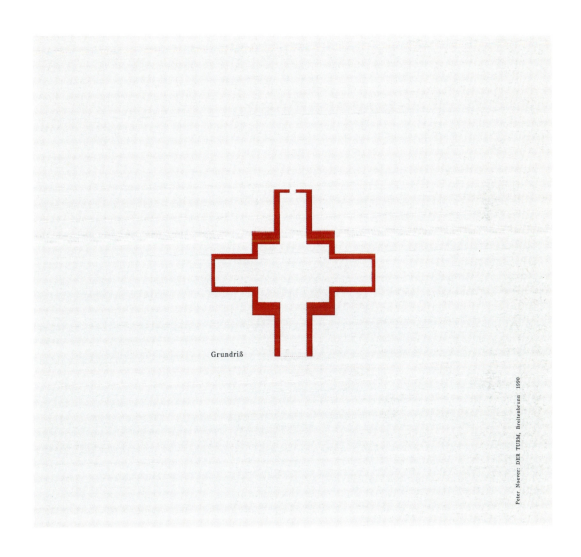

Der Turm, Grundriß, Ausgangsüberlegung, 1990 / The Tower, Ground-plan, first stage, 1990

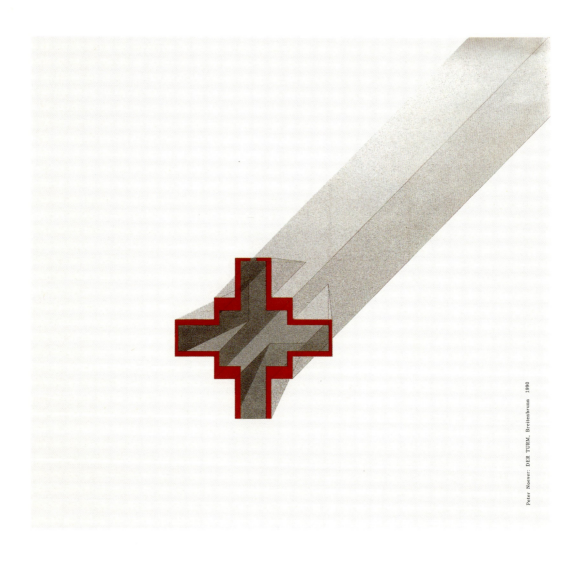

Der Turm, Grundriß / The Tower, Ground-plan

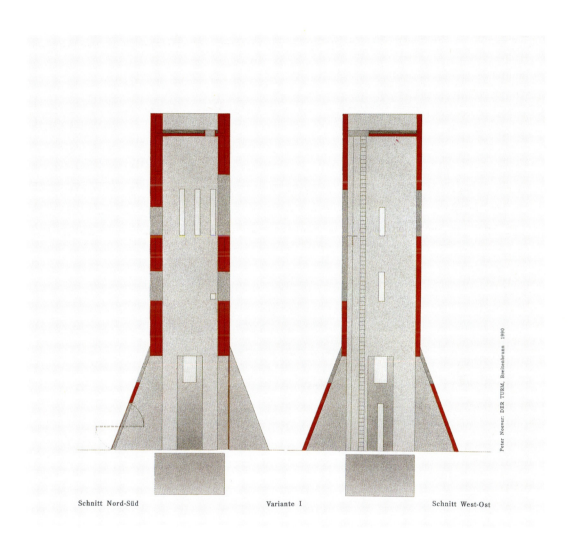

Variante I (Aussichtsturm), Schnitt Nord-Süd, Schnitt West-Ost / Stage I (Observation Tower), Section North-South, Section West-East

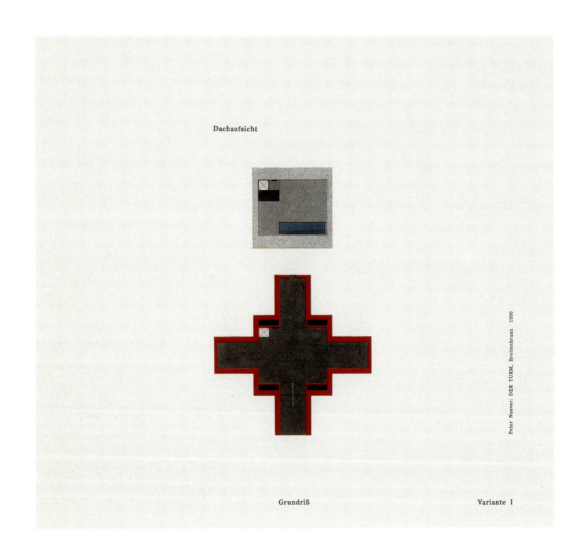

Variante I, Grundriß / Stage I, Ground-plan

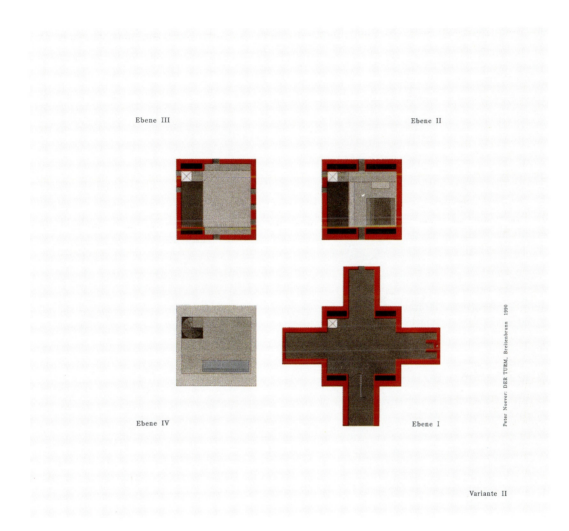

Variante II (Wohnturm), Grundriß mit Horizontalschnitten / Stage II (Tower for Living), Ground-plan with horizontal Sections

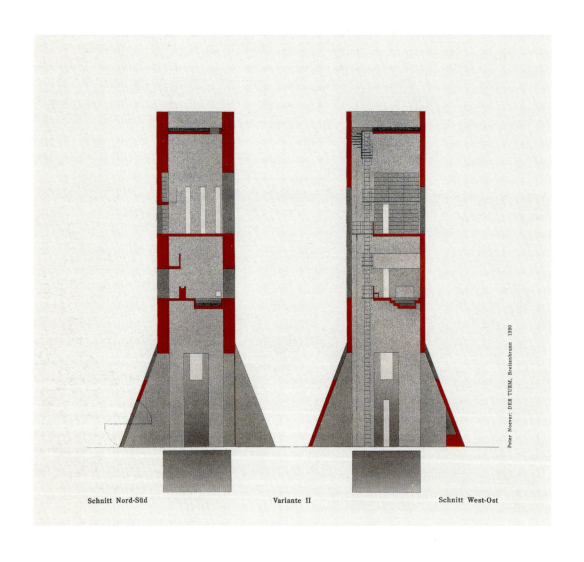

Variante II, Schnitt Nord-Süd, Schnitt West-Ost / Stage II, Section North-South, Section West-East

Der Turm, Variante II, Innenansicht mit Zwischendecken, „Lastenaufzug" und hängendem Treppenelement (Modell aus Holz, Maßstab 1:50, Höhe 50 cm) / The Tower, Interior View with Floor Levels, "Freight elevator" and hanging Stairs (model of wood, scale 1:50, height 50 cm)

Seite 82/83 / Page 82/83: Der Turm, 4 Ansichten (Eingang: Süden) / The Tower, 4 Side Views (Entrance: South)

Süd   West

Nord   Ost

Geboren 1. Mai 1941, Designer.
Seit 1986 Direktor des Österreichischen Museums für angewandte Kunst (MAK), Wien; 1988/89 Gastprofessor für Museologie an der Hochschule für angewandte Kunst und seit 1975 Lehrbeauftragter für Designanalyse an der Akademie der bildenden Künste, Wien. Seit 1982 Herausgeber der Architekturzeitschrift UMRISS. Noever publiziert laufend Artikel über Kunst, Design und Architektur in in- und ausländischen Zeitungen und Zeitschriften.
Verschiedene Medienarbeiten, wie u. a. 1984 ein 16-mm-Design-Film „Endstation Supermarkt" im Auftrag des Österreichischen Fernsehens (ORF).
Baut seit 1971 an seinem Landschafts-Architektur-Projekt „Die Grube" in Breitenbrunn/Burgenland, Ostösterreich. Verschiedene Architekturprojekte, wie u. a. Entwurf des MAK-Terrassenplateaus für den Museumsgarten, 1989 (Realisierung 1990/91).
Gestalter von Ausstellungen im In- und Ausland (u. a. „Land in Sicht – Österreichische Kunst im 20. Jahrhundert", Budapest 1989). Zahlreiche Entwürfe, teilweise in Serie hergestellter Produkte. Ausstellungsdesign und graphische Entwürfe. Mitglied des „Beirates für bildende Kunst" im Bundesministerium für Unterricht, Kunst und Sport (1987–1989).
Konsulententätigkeit für Planungsgrundlagen, zuletzt 1985, 1989 und 1991 in Havanna (gemeinsam mit Carl Pruscha – C.P.P.N.), im Auftrag des Kubanischen Kulturministeriums.
Zahlreiche Gastvorträge an verschiedenen Universitäten, wie TU Wien, TU Graz, University of California, Berkeley, Ball State University, Muncie/Indiana, USA. Herausgeber von Kunst- und Architekturpublikationen (u. a. „Wiener Architekturgespräche", Verlag Ernst & Sohn, Berlin 1991, „Architektur im AufBRUCH", Prestel Verlag, München 1991).
Noever lebt in Wien.

Peter Noever

Born May 1, 1941, Designer.
From 1986 until the present, Director of the Austrian Museum for Applied Arts (MAK) in Vienna; in 1988/89 Guest Professor for Museology at the University for Applied Arts, and since 1975 Guest Professor for Design Analysis at the Academy of Fine Arts in Vienna. From 1982 on, editor of the architectural magazine UMRISS. Noever consistently publishes articles on art, design, and architecture in domestic and foreign newspapers and magazines. Various media projects, among them in 1984 a 16 mm Design Film called "Endstation Supermarkt" commissioned by Austrian Television (ORF).
Has worked since 1971 on his landscape architecture project "Die Grube" ("The Pit") in Breitenbrunn/Burgenland, Austria.
Various architectural projects, including the design of the MAK Terrace Plateau for the museum courtyard in 1988 (completion in 1990/91). Design of exhibitions in Austria and abroad, among them "Land in Sicht – Österreichische Kunst im 20. Jahrhundert" ("Land in Sight – Austrian Art in the 20th Century") in Budapest, 1989. Numerous designs, some of which were done for product series. Exhibition design and graphic layouts.
Member of the "Council for Fine Arts" in the Federal Ministry for Education, Art, and Sports (1987–1989).
Consultant for Fundamental Planning, most recently in 1985, 1989 and 1991 in Havana (together with Carl Pruscha – C.P.P.N.), commissioned by the Cuban Ministry of Culture. Guest lectures at various universities, including the Technical Universities of Vienna and Graz, the University of California, Berkeley, Ball State University, Muncie/Indiana, USA. Editor of art and architectural publications, including "Wiener Architekturgespräche" ("Viennese Architectural Discussions") from the Ernst & Sohn Publishing House, Berlin 1991, "Architektur im AufBRUCH", Prestel Verlag, München 1991.
Noever lives in Vienna.

BIBLIOGRAPHY / THE PIT

Magazines (among others)

Domus, Nr. 529, Milano 1973
Transparent, Nr. 11/12, Wien 1973
Baumeister, Nr. 1, München 1974
Design, London, März 1974
MD Möbel Interior Design, Nr. 5, Leinfelden, BRD, 1974
Casabella, Milano, Dezember 1974
Casa Vogue, Milano, April 1975
Bauforum, Nr. 57/58, Wien 1976
Archtetyp, Nr. 2, San Francisco 1979
Gran Bazaar, Milano, Oktober 1985

Books and Film (among others)

Friedrich Achleitner, *Österreichische Architektur im 20. Jahrhundert, Band II*
Residenz Verlag, Salzburg 1983

Site, *De-Architecture*
New York 1985

Günther Feuerstein, *Visionäre Architektur, Wien 1958/1988*
Ernst & Sohn, Berlin 1988

Andrea Schurian, *TV-Film (35 Minuten): Die Grube*
ORF, Wien, 28. Oktober 1988

Ergänzend zum Ausstellungskatalog (ISBN 3-901127-01-1) ist eine Fotodokumentation „Die Grube" (Format 30×40,5 cm, ISBN 3-901127-02-X) erschienen.

A Photodocumentation "The Pit" (format 30×40.5 cm, ISBN 3-901127-02-X) has been published in addition to the Exhibition Catalogue (ISBN 3-901127-01-1).

*Besonderer Dank für die Realisierung meines Projektes (1972–1990) gebührt /
Special Thanks for their Support in the Realization of my Project (1972–1990) to*

meiner Mutter, Mimy Noever

*Michael Hasenöhrl
Wilfried Hicke
Christa Krammer
Hilde und Siegfried Mader
Werner Schalk
Richard Schiwampl
Josef Scherbl
Anton Siegl
Hans Sipötz
Wolfgang Strobach
Emmerich Waha*

Bildnachweis / List of Illustration

Ixy Noever: Seite/page 57
Katarina Noever: Seite/page 50
Peter Noever: Seite/page 40, 41, 50, 52, 60, 61, 62, 63, 64, 65, 66, 67, 68, 69
Barbara Rhode: Seite/page 84
Brian Spence: Seite/page 8, 13, 14, 19
Peter Strobl: Seite/page 5, 34
Gerald Zugmann: Seite/page 30, 31, 32, 33, 35, 36, 37, 38, 39, 42, 43, 44, 45, 46, 47, 48, 49, 52, 53, 55, 58, 59, 66, 67, 71